NO ROOM FOR FRANCIE

Maryann Macdonald
Illustrated by Eileen Christelow

Hyperion Books for Children
New York

For my brother, Tom Vanderwerp

—M.M.

Printed in the United States of America.
For information address
Hyperion Books for Children,
114 Fifth Avenue
New York, New York 10011-5690

FIRST EDITION
1 3 5 7 9 10 8 6 4 2

Library of Congress Cataloging-in-Publication Data
Macdonald, Maryann.
No room for Francie/Maryann Macdonald; illustrated by Eileen Christelow—1st ed.
p. cm.
Summary: There are six children in the O'Leary family, and when
her Comics Club needs a place to meet, Francie seems to be
the only one with no special place of her very own.
ISBN 0-7868-0032-1 (trade)—0-7868-1081-5 (pbk.)
[1. Family life—Fiction. 2. Brothers and sisters—Fiction.
3. Clubs—Fiction.] I. Christelow, Eileen, ill; II. Title.
PZ7.M1486No 1995
[Fic]—dc20 94-8596 CIP AC

Chapter One

"Now then, class," said Sister Ursula Agnes. "Is everyone ready to do some good, hard work?"

Francie O'Leary wasn't ready. She was playing dot-to-dot with the freckles on her arm.

Her best friend, Stella Zujak, wasn't ready either. She was designing a dress for Brenda Starr.

Her other friend, Chiffon Brown, wasn't ready either. She was dancing to a made-up song in her head.

But Sister Ursula Agnes, their second-grade teacher, was ready. She loved hard work.

"Right!" she said. "Let's begin."

She wrote a series of numbers on the blackboard.

Francie sighed. It was Friday afternoon. She couldn't wait for three o'clock. She and Stella were going to Chiffon's house. They were going to play and have FUN!

But Francie picked up her pencil. It scratched across the paper. What was five plus eight? Who knows? thought Francie. Who cares?

She started playing dot-to-dot again.

"Frances!" said a chilling voice. "What are you doing?"

Francie felt prickles creep up her

back. "Nothing, Sister," she said.

"NOTHING!" bellowed Sister Ursula Agnes. Her eyes flashed behind her steel glasses. Lies upset her.

"You are drawing on your arm!" The big nun hovered over Francie like a huge black cloud.

"I'm sorry, Sister," said Francie.

"Don't let it happen again," Sister Ursula Agnes said. "I don't give second chances." Then she whirled around.

"NICO BONFIGLIO," she said in slow, scary tones, "there will be no spitballs in my class." She rapped Nicky's desk with her big knuckles.

Francie shivered. How did her teacher know what was happening behind her back?

Brrrrrrrrrring! The bell at last! Everybody jumped out of their seats.

They pushed out the door.

Francie met Stella and Chiffon outside. Annabelle Carter, meanie and sneak, was with them.

"Nobody told me *Francie* was coming," said Annabelle. She rolled her big blue eyes. She tossed her shiny blond hair. "What's that on your arm, Francie?" she asked. "Spiderwebs?"

Francie extended her arm. "No, Annabelle," she said. "I was drawing your picture. Like it?"

Annabelle stuck out her tongue at Francie. Francie crossed her eyes at Annabelle. "Nobody told me that *you* were coming, either," Francie said.

Chiffon shrugged. "Annabelle's got money," she said. "She's going to buy us candy at the 7-Eleven."

She nudged Chiffon. "We've got *plans*," said Francie. "Remember?"

Annabelle waved some green bills. "Plans change," she said. "Come on, Stella and Chiffon. Let's go."

"Not without Francie," said Stella.

"I don't think I've got enough money for *her*," Annabelle said.

"I'll share my candy with Francie," said Stella.

"Me, too," said Chiffon.

Annabelle sighed. "Okay," she said. "I guess I can buy something for her." She glared at Francie. "Are you coming or not?"

"I'm coming," said Francie. She detested Annabelle. But she loved candy.

"Let's get Junior Mints!" said Stella.

"And Butterfingers!" said Chiffon.

"And comic books!" said Francie.

"Yeah!" they all shouted. They ran all the way to the 7-Eleven.

Chapter Two

The girls placed all the things they wanted on the counter. Chiffon had a Catwoman comic and some bubble gum. Stella had an Uncle Scrooge and some Junior Mints. Francie had a Little Archie and a Butterfinger.

But Annabelle had all the money.

"Add it up," said the clerk. "Three dollars is not enough."

"Let's see," said Annabelle. "We'll leave out Francie's comic. Then I'll pick out candy for everyone."

She gave Chiffon her bubble gum. She gave Stella her Junior Mints. And she gave Francie one big piece of hard red candy.

"Hey," said Francie, "everyone got what they wanted but me!"

Annabelle shrugged. "It's my money," she said.

It was true. What could Francie say?

She put the red candy in her mouth. Her tongue started to burn. Her eyes started to water. The big piece of red candy was a fireball!

But Annabelle was watching her. So Francie sucked on that fireball all the way to Chiffon's. She pretended she liked it.

"Hey, girls," said Chiffon's mom when they came in. "Hungry?"

She made them hot chocolate with tiny marshmallows floating on top.

"Mmmmmmm . . . ," said Francie, sucking a marshmallow. They never had tiny marshmallows at her house.

"Can we have potato chips, too, Mama?" asked Chiffon.

"Sure, baby," said Mrs. Brown. She gave them each a fun-size bag of potato chips. Chiffon's eyes gleamed.

The girls took everything into Chiffon's room. They ate sitting on Chiffon's bed.

Chiffon's bedspread had ruffles all around. She had a dressing table, too, with a skirt. On the dressing table were tiny shiny bottles.

"They're samples," Chiffon said. "My mom gets them at work." Chiffon's mom was a makeup lady.

Francie fingered the shiny bedspread. Chiffon was lucky. She had so many nice things. She even had a beautiful room all her own. Francie had to share a room with her sister and brother. And Francie's mom never bought fun-size anything. She had six kids. So she bought giant-size everything.

"Want to play dress-up?" Chiffon asked.

Annabelle wrinkled her nose. "Dress-up is boring," she said.

"How about Barbies?" asked Stella.

"Barbies are for *babies*!" said Annabelle.

"I know," said Francie. "Let's play Archie!"

"I get to be Veronica!" said Annabelle.

"I'm Betty!" said Chiffon.

"I'll be Midge," said Stella.

"No fair!" said Francie. "That means

I have to be a boy!"

"You can be Miss Grundy," said Annabelle.

"No way," said Chiffon. "Who wants to be a teacher?"

So they had to take turns being Archie, Reggie, and Jughead.

"I've got to go home now," said Stella at five o'clock.

"Let's play Archie again next Friday . . . we can have a comics club!" said Francie.

"Let's!" said Stella. "We can meet every Friday."

"And eat!" said Chiffon.

"And read comics!" said Annabelle.

Francie was excited. "Let's meet at my house next week," she said.

"All-right!" said Chiffon. She

snapped her fingers.

Francie tried snapping her fingers, too, on the way home. She wasn't very good at it. But it seemed like the right thing to do when you were happy. And Francie was happy.

She and her friends were going to have a *club*! Maybe they would make membership cards! Maybe they would devise a secret code word to get into meetings! Maybe someday they would even build a clubhouse!

It was too bad they were stuck with Annabelle. But it would still be fun. Francie was going to make sure of that.

Chapter Three

"Mom! I'm home!" yelled Francie. She couldn't wait to tell Mom about the comics club.

"I'm in the kitchen, Francie," Mom yelled back. "Can you help me give the twins a bath?"

The twins were only two months old. They were very demanding.

Tobias lay on a towel at the edge of the kitchen sink. Francie held him down with one hand. She soaped him with the other. Mom rinsed Mathias off in the sink.

"Look, Mom," said Francie. "Tobias knows how to blow bubbles."

Mom smiled her tired smile. "Here, Francie, let's swap babies," she said. She lifted Mathias out of the sink.

Francie switched babies with Mom. She wrapped Mathias in a soft towel. She smelled his baby smell. "MMM-mmm!" she said.

"Mom," said Francie, "I'm in a new club."

"Oh?" said Mom.

"Yes," said Francie. "A comics club. With Chiffon and Stella. And Annabelle Carter."

"That's nice," said Mom.

"We're going to meet here next Friday," said Francie.

"Great," said Mom. "I'll make you a big bowl of popcorn."

"Mom," said Francie, "I don't want a big bowl of popcorn. I don't want anything we have to share."

Mom blinked. "Why not?" she said.

"I'm sick of sharing," Francie explained. "I like to have things that are all mine."

"Hmmm," said Mom. "Like what?"

"Like Cracker Jack," said Francie. "And juice in little boxes. Things like that."

"Well," said Mom, "I suppose I could buy some Cracker Jack. And juice in boxes. Since it's so important to you."

Francie was happy. "Thanks, Mom," she said.

She kissed Tobias's soft baby hair. She kissed Mathias's fat baby foot.

Now she just had to find a place for the club meeting.

Francie helped Mom dress the twins. They were warm and sleepy.

"Let's put them in bed," Mom whispered.

So Francie tiptoed up the stairs carrying Tobias. Mom tiptoed right behind her carrying Mathias.

Francie elbowed open the door to the babies' room. The room was jampacked. Jo Jo, last year's baby, was napping in her crib in the corner. Francie kicked her way through toys and clothes. She lay Tobias down carefully in his baby basket. Mom lay Mathias down carefully in his basket. Then they tiptoed silently out the door and into Mom's room.

"Whew!" said Mom. "We did it!" She slumped in her desk chair and closed her eyes.

Francie looked around Mom's room. It was neat and tidy. The dresser had Mom's jewelry box and silver mirror on it. The windows had fluffy curtains.

"Mom," said Francie, "could I have my club meeting in here on Friday?"

"Francie," said Mom, "you know I don't like kids playing in this room."

"Why not?" said Francie.

"Because," said Mom, "it's a private place for me and Dad."

"Hmmph!" said Francie. "I wish *I* had a private place!"

But all she had was one crummy room and she had to share it with Dolores and Ambrose.

Chapter Four

Francie opened the door to her room. She was hoping no one was there. But Dolores was there, playing with her dollhouse.

It was big, with real glass windows. Dad had made it last Christmas.

Dolores was carefully cutting out some wallpaper for the dolls' dining room. She pasted it neatly on one wall.

Francie peeked in. The dollhouse was neat and perfect, just like Dolores.

Francie flopped down on her bed.

"Dolores," she said, "I'm having a club meeting in our room. Next Friday after school."

"How many people?" asked Dolores.

"Four," said Francie.

"I hope they're quiet," said Dolores.

"Why?" asked Francie.

"You know there's always at least one baby asleep next door," said Dolores.

Francie sighed. Dolores was right. How could she have a Comics Club meeting with babies next door?

Francie pulled her quilt over her head. She sat in her tent and thought.

"I know!" she said at last. "I'll make a big tent with sheets and blankets. We can have our club meeting in it."

Dolores looked up. "What if it rains?"

Dolores was so practical. But she was

right. Francie would have to try the basement.

But Ambrose was in the basement, as usual, taking things apart.

Romeo and Juliet, Ambrose's hamsters, lived there, too. Romeo was running in his hamster wheel. "*Screeee-screeee!*" went the wheel. It was an awful noise. But Juliet didn't seem to mind. She was sleeping peacefully on a pile of chewed-up newspaper.

"Ambrose," said Francie, "can I use the basement on Friday?"

Ambrose didn't look up. "Friday?" he said. "Sure." He straightened his glasses. Ambrose's glasses were always crooked.

"*Screeeeee-screeeeee,*" went the wheel.

"One more thing," said Francie. "Can you take your hamsters upstairs that day?"

21

"Mom won't let me take them up-stairs," said Ambrose. He sniffed and wrinkled his nose. "She says they smell."

Smell? thought Francie. Maybe they did. She didn't want her friends to think her house smelled. But where else was there to have a club meeting?

She looked around the basement. She saw the furnace, the washtubs, the cedar closet. . . .

The cedar closet! She used to play in there when she was in kindergarten.

Francie jumped up and ran to the door. She reached up and switched on the light. The closet was empty! It was big and cool. It smelled like fresh wood. It had a wall of shelves where they could keep their comics. Best of all, it was private!

"Dad just moved his tools from there into the garage," said Ambrose. "Why don't you go ask him if you can use it?"

But Francie was already on her way up the stairs.

Francie found Dad in the garage. He was whistling. He was hanging up his tools, one by one. Dad loved his tools.

"My Comics Club meeting is here next Friday," Francie explained. "Can we use the cedar closet for our clubhouse?"

"Friday?" said Dad. "I don't think so, Pumpkin. They're delivering the freezer on Wednesday."

"The freezer?" said Francie.

Dad nodded. "We need a big freezer now with so many people in the house. And there's nowhere to put it but that closet."

The door from the kitchen opened, "Keep an eye on Jo Jo," said Mom. She lifted Jo Jo through the door. Ernestina, the dog, trotted along behind. Ernestina and Jo Jo went everywhere together. They both thought Jo Jo was a dog.

Francie was thinking fast. "We could put the freezer out here in the garage," she said. "Lots of people do that."

But Dad shook his head. "I'm setting up my workshop here, Francie. There just won't be room for a freezer."

Jo Jo crawled across the cement floor. Ernestina followed behind. Jo Jo went right over to an open paint can.

But Dad swung Jo Jo up into the air. "No!" he said sharply. He handed Jo Jo to Francie. "Be a good girl and take Jo Jo out to the swing," he said. "She might get hurt in here."

Francie slammed out the door with Jo Jo. She dumped Jo Jo into the swing. She gave her a hard push. Jo Jo yelled happily. Ernestina ran back and forth with the swing.

Dad was always building things, thought Francie. He built the swing for Jo Jo. He built the dollhouse for Dolores. He built the hamster cage for Ambrose. He even built a doghouse for Ernestina.

Francie walked over to Ernestina's house. She crawled through the door. It was snug inside. But there wasn't enough room for a club.

Francie sighed. Everyone else had a private space. She stared around the yard. And there, in the corner, she saw the shed.

Francie walked over to it. Spiderwebs hung from the ceiling. Francie knocked over a broken flowerpot. Hundreds of roly-poly bugs tumbled into balls.

But the shed had real windows and a real door. Maybe she could make it into a clubhouse. She would just have to try. There was nowhere else.

Chapter Five

"What were you doing out in that old shed?" Mom asked Francie at dinner.

Francie swallowed a big mouthful of spaghetti. "I was fixing it up," she said. "I'm making it into a clubhouse."

"Nice clubhouse," said Ambrose. "Bug City."

"Ugh," said Dolores. "I wouldn't set foot in that place." She shivered.

"Do you think the shed is a good place to play with your friends?" asked Mom.

"No," said Francie. "But all the good

places around here are taken. I just want *one* private place for me and my friends."

Dad nodded. "I can understand that."

Jo Jo was stuffing spaghetti into her mouth with her hands. Mom tried to show her how to use a fork.

"NO!" yelled Jo Jo.

"She wants to eat by herself," said Ambrose. "She doesn't want any help."

"Well, *I* could use some help," said Francie. But nobody took the hint.

So first thing Saturday morning, Francie had to ask for help. Dolores was good at cleaning. Francie asked her first. But Dolores was busy sewing.

"Please," Francie begged. "It's a big job. I need help."

"Francie," said Dolores, "I *told* you I hate bugs. Ask Ambrose."

27

Ambrose didn't hate bugs. But he said he was busy, too.

"You don't look that busy to me," said Francie.

Ambrose was fooling around with a piece of old rope. "I'm thinking," said Ambrose. He tied a big knot in the rope.

"Come on," said Francie. "You can think while we clean out the shed."

"Nope," said Ambrose. He untied the knot. "I think better in the basement."

Francie sighed. It was no use arguing with Ambrose. She went to find Dad.

Dad was sanding something. The sander made a lot of noise.

"CAN YOU HELP ME WITH THE SHED?" Francie yelled.

"WHAT'S WRONG WITH YOUR HEAD?" Dad yelled back.

"NOTHING!" Francie yelled. "I

NEED HELP WITH THE SHED!"

"I'LL HELP YOU MOVE YOUR BED LATER, OKAY?" Dad yelled.

Francie gave up.

She went to the kitchen to get an apple. Mom was there feeding the twins. "Mom," she said, "do you have time to help me clean out the shed?"

Mom had a baby bottle in each hand. Her hair was in her eyes. "Francie," she said, "does it look like I have time?"

"I guess not," said Francie. She tucked Mom's hair behind her ear.

"Thanks," said Mom. "Do me a favor and watch Jo Jo for a while."

"Mom," said Francie, "can't somebody else watch her for a change?"

Mom didn't answer. She just looked at Francie.

"All right," said Francie, "I'll do it."

Jo Jo was in the living room, wiping applesauce on the TV. Ernestina was licking it off.

Francie took Jo Jo outside and belted her into her stroller. Ernestina stood whining at the screen door.

"Okay, okay, you can come, too," said Francie. She opened the door and Ernestina bounded down the steps.

Francie pushed Jo Jo's stroller up to the shed. "There," she said. "Now you sit still while I clean the shed."

But Jo Jo didn't want to sit still. She wanted to push her stroller. She yelled until she got her way.

Then Ernestina wanted to fetch sticks. She whined until Francie threw one.

It's not fair, thought Francie. Everyone in this family gets their own way. Everyone except me!

Chapter Six

The next morning, all the O'Learys were going to church. Francie didn't feel like going. "I think my stomach hurts," she said.

Mom looked at Dad.

"I'll stay home with her," Dad offered. He liked to read the newspaper on Sundays.

"Okay," said Mom. "You can stay home this time. But don't get out of bed."

So Francie stayed in bed. She heard the car drive away. Then the house got too quiet.

Francie knew she shouldn't bother Dad. And she knew she was supposed to stay in bed. But she snuck down to the basement. She got Romeo and Juliet out of their cage. Then she tiptoed back upstairs with them. She made a tent in her bed. She let Romeo and Juliet explore inside the tent.

The three of them were having a good time playing until Francie heard the car pull up outside. She didn't have time to take the hamsters back downstairs. So she dropped the hamsters inside Dolores's dollhouse. Then she pulled the covers up to her nose.

Ambrose came in the bedroom and took off his jacket. "Too bad you've got a stomachache," he said. "Mom got doughnuts on the way home."

Francie peeked out over the blanket. "What kind?" she asked.

"All kinds," said Ambrose. "Jelly. Chocolate. Glazed."

Glazed! That was Francie's favorite.

She jumped out of bed. "I feel a lot better now," she said to Ambrose.

"I bet you do," he said.

"Mom," said Francie. "I feel better." Mom put her hand on Francie's forehead. "Hmmm . . . ," she said. "No temperature. It must have been something you ate."

Francie nodded. "I'm hungry now." She sat down and began to lick the glaze off a big doughnut. Mom stirred cream into her coffee. Everything was peaceful until Ambrose burst in.

"Romeo and Juliet are gone!" he said. "I can't find them anywhere."

Uh-oh, thought Francie. She had meant to put the hamsters back before anyone noticed. But now it was too late.

"I can't understand it," Ambrose said. "I always make sure the door is latched." He sounded as if he might cry.

Dad came in. "Never mind, Son," he said. "We'll find them." He put his arm around Ambrose.

Francie squirmed in her seat. "I'll look upstairs," she offered. She slid off the bench and ran up to the bedroom.

Francie went over to the dollhouse. She opened the front door carefully. "Romeo?" she whispered. "Juliet?"

She peeked in the kitchen window. The hamsters had tried to eat the plaster food. They had knocked over the china cabinet. Dishes lay broken on the floor.

Francie swung open the front of the dollhouse on its hinges. Romeo and Juliet had wrecked the place. They had clawed the new wallpaper. They had chewed on the sofa. They had scratched up the windows. Then they must have escaped up the chimney. Dolores would be furious!

Chapter Seven

"We still can't find Romeo and Juliet," Francie told the girls at lunch the next day. "Dad thinks they're trapped behind the walls. Ernestina keeps sniffing the heating vents."

Annabelle shivered, "Rodents!" she said. "Living in the walls. How creepy."

"Hamsters aren't rodents!" said Chiffon.

"They're sweet little furry animals," added Stella. "And they're lost."

"Ambrose is really upset," Francie went on. "He spends all his time trying to lure them out with M&M's."

Annabelle sniffed. "That brother of yours must be weird," she said.

Francie gave Annabelle a dirty look. Ambrose *was* weird. Francie knew it. But she didn't like other people to say so.

"Dolores is mad, too," she said. "She won't talk to me. And Mom's making me do the dishes every night this week. That's for getting out of bed when she said not to."

"Well," said Annabelle. "Francie's house sounds gloomy. Let's have Comics Club on Friday at my house. I've got a VCR." She looked at Francie sideways. "Do you have a VCR, Francie?"

Francie swallowed hard. "I've got something better," she said.

"Like what?" said Annabelle.

Francie hated her. "I've got a private clubhouse," Francie said.

"I bet," said Annabelle.

But Stella was excited. "Can I come and see it after school?"

"I guess so," Francie said.

Of course Annabelle wanted to come, too. Francie was stuck. She walked home from school with Stella and Annabelle as slowly as possible.

"Is that it?" said Annabelle when the girls were standing at the door to the shed. "What a wreck!"

"It's not exactly *finished* yet, Annabelle," Francie said. "You have to use your imagination."

Stella nodded. Francie took a deep breath and opened the door.

The girls looked at the dust. They looked at the broken junk and the

spiderwebs.

Annabelle laughed out loud. "You call this a clubhouse?" she said. "What a dump!"

"Oh, go home, Annabelle," said Francie.

"Don't worry!" said Annabelle. She stuck her nose in the air and stalked off.

"It does need a little fixing up," said Stella.

"Oh, Stella," said Francie. "It's awful. I shouldn't have bragged. But I just couldn't let Annabelle have her way. This place is a mess. My whole family is mad at me. And I'll never be able to finish this by Friday."

Francie sat down in the rusted old wheelbarrow. She started to cry. Stella sat down next to her. She put her arm around Francie.

Then the wheelbarrow crashed over

backward. Stella and Francie landed in the flowerpots. Spiderwebs drifted down into their faces. Stella started to giggle. Francie did, too. It felt funny to be upside down in floating spiderwebs. Stella and Francie laughed until their stomachs hurt.

At last, Stella stood up. She brushed the dirt off her dress. "You know what?" she said. "I'll help you fix up the clubhouse. We'll make it really great."

Francie looked at Stella. What a good friend! "You're right," said Francie. "We'll make it into the best clubhouse ever!"

She wiped her eyes on her shirt. And she got up and started piling junk in the wheelbarrow.

Chapter Eight

"I don't know what I'd do without you, Stella," said Francie.

It was Tuesday. The girls had spent two afternoons cleaning up the shed. Now they were taping cardboard over a broken windowpane.

"Dolores won't help me at all," Francie went on. "All she does is sew, sew, sew! All Ambrose does is look for his hamsters. And my dad just works in the garage."

"What about your mom?" asked

Stella.

"Babies!" said Francie. "Babies are all she cares about."

Stella nodded. "Vincent is four," she said, "and my mom *still* thinks he's a baby. I have to watch him tomorrow after school, so I can't come over and help you."

"Never mind," said Francie. "We can finish up on Thursday."

But on Thursday Stella couldn't come over, either.

"I'm *really* sorry," she said. "It's Vincent again. If I don't take care of him today, I can't come to the club meeting tomorrow."

"That's okay," Francie lied. She didn't want Stella to feel bad.

But it wasn't okay. Francie needed

HELP!

She went to Dolores. "Please," she said. "There's still so much to do and my club meeting is tomorrow!"

"Sorry, Francie," said Dolores.

"What are you sewing that's so important?" asked Francie.

"It's a secret," said Dolores. She was so calm that Francie felt like kicking her. Instead she went to find Ambrose.

"Ambrose, you've got to help me," said Francie. "I'll never finish alone."

Ambrose was building a hamster trap. "No way," he said, "I've got to find Romeo and Juliet. It's a matter of life and death!"

Francie ran upstairs to find Mom. She was rocking both twins at once. They were fussy. "I've got my hands full here," Mom said.

Francie could see it was true. Dad wouldn't be home until six o'clock. She would just have to finish the clubhouse alone.

Francie dragged the tools out. Then she swept and dusted. She got very dirty. But the shed got clean.

When the shed was clean, it looked too empty. Francie got some pink chalk. She made patterns on the floor. She put some wildflowers in a glass jar on the window ledge. Finally, she got some blue paint and painted the words "COMICS CLUBHOUSE" on the door.

At last the clubhouse was done! Francie sat on the floor and hugged her knees.

Tomorrow was Friday. The juice boxes and the Cracker Jack were waiting. The clubhouse was ready. Everything was going to be perfect . . . wasn't it?

Chapter Nine

Friday at last! The class was doing math again. Everyone but Francie, that is.

Francie was drawing a picture of her new clubhouse. She was inside with her friends.

Ambrose, Dolores, and Jo Jo were outside. So were Mom and Dad. They all wanted to come in. But the door was locked shut.

Francie was just starting to draw Ernestina when Sister Ursula Agnes picked up her picture. "DRAWING AGAIN, FRANCES?" she boomed. "During MATH?"

Francie hung her head. She was dead. Sister Ursula Agnes did not give second chances.

"See me after school, Frances," she said.

After school? "Not today!" said Francie.

"*TODAY!*" said the big nun. "Now get started on this math."

Francie picked up her pencil. She stared at the numbers. But all she could think about was her club meeting! What would happen?

A note dropped onto Francie's desk. It said:

Now we don't have to go to your crummy clubhouse. We can all go to my house instead.

—Annabelle

That turkey! thought Francie. She stuffed the note in her pocket. But then she had an idea. Slowly, she reached toward Stella's desk. If she got caught, there would be more trouble! She dropped the note onto Stella's desk.

Stella read the note. She looked at Francie. "Don't worry," she whispered.

Francie felt better.

The bell rang.

Sister Ursula Agnes crossed her large hands in front of her. "Come here, please, Frances," she said.

Francie walked up to the front of the room. Her picture was right on the desk.

"Now, Frances," said the nun, "tell me about this picture."

It was no use lying. Sister Ursula Agnes hated lies. Besides, if you told one lie, you always had to tell more.

"It's my family, Sister," Francie said.

"They can't come into my clubhouse."

"Why is that?" asked the nun.

"Because I'm mad at them," said Francie. "They were all too busy to help me fix it up."

"Ah," said Sister Ursula Agnes. "I always wanted a room of my own, too."

Francie blinked. "You did?"

"Certainly," said the nun. "I had nine brothers and sisters."

Nine! thought Francie. That was worse than five. "Did you get your own room?"

"It would have taken a miracle in our house," said Sister Ursula Agnes.

Francie nodded. "Mine, too," she said.

The big nun folded up the drawing. She put it in an envelope. She's going to send it to my parents, thought Francie. Then I'll be in even more trouble!

Chapter Ten

But Sister Ursula Agnes handed the drawing back to Francie. Then she wrote a sentence on the blackboard: "I will not draw in math class."

"Copy this," she said, "ten times, please."

Francie took the drawing. She copied the dull sentence as fast as she could. Then she handed her paper back.

"Hmm...," said the nun, "sloppy work."

Rats, thought Francie. She's going to make me do it again.

But the nun did not. Instead, she said, "You may go now, Frances. I will pray for a miracle. But no more drawing in math class!"

Francie ran out into the hallway. Her friends weren't waiting for her. But in her cubby was a note:

Meet us at the clubhouse.

—Stella

Hooray! Francie grabbed her jacket. She ran all the way home.

Mom was in the kitchen, making popcorn.

"I'm afraid everyone's eaten all the Cracker Jack," she said. "Your friends shared it."

Oh no! thought Francie. Had her friends had to share with her sisters and brothers?

"Mom!" said Francie. "I don't want the whole family at my club meeting!"

"It couldn't be helped," said Mom. "It was up to us to entertain your friends. Why did you have to stay after school?"

Francie didn't answer. She ran outside.

Her friends were all in the clubhouse—but so were Dolores, Ambrose, Jo Jo, Tobias, Mathias, and Ernestina.

Francie barged in. "Out!" she yelled. "This is my clubhouse. I fixed it up myself."

"All right," said Dolores.

"Dolores," said Annabelle, "let me show you how to do handstands." And she tagged along after Dolores.

"Come on, Jo Jo," said Ambrose. "I'll give you a wheelbarrow ride."

"Can I have one, too?" asked Chiffon.

Chiffon and Ernestina ran out the door after Ambrose.

"Waaaaaah!" yelled Tobias.

"Nyaaaaah!" yelled Mathias.

"Francie!" said Stella. "You scared them." Out went Stella with the baby carriage and the babies.

"Wait!" said Francie. "I didn't mean for *everyone* to go."

But no one was listening.

Francie ran to Chiffon. "Chiffon," she said, "let's play Catwoman."

"Not now," said Chiffon. She was climbing into the wheelbarrow. Ambrose gave Chiffon a bumpy ride.

"Stella," said Francie. "Please come

back."

But Stella put her finger to her lips. "Shhh!" she said. She was rocking the babies.

"Annabelle," Francie said, "come on back to the clubhouse."

"No way," said Annabelle. She did a handstand for Dolores.

So Francie went back to the shed by herself. She sat down in a corner.

There was Cracker Jack scattered all over. The pink chalk was all smudged. And the wildflowers on the windowsill were wilted and ruined. Just like Francie's club meeting.

Chapter Eleven

For a long time, Francie sat on the club-house floor. Outside, she could hear her friends. They were shouting and laughing with her family. They didn't need her or her clubhouse.

Finally, the door creaked open.

"We've got to go home now, Francie," said Stella.

"We had the *coolest* time!" said Chiffon.

"I'll be back next week," said Annabelle, "if Dolores is here."

Francie didn't say anything.

"Bye-bye, Francie," said Stella.

"Bye, girl," said Chiffon.

Annabelle slammed the door behind her.

"I thought you said Annabelle was a total creep," said Dolores that night. "She's really good at handstands."

"Chiffon is the most fun girl I've ever met." said Ambrose. "Does she like hamsters?"

Francie pretended she was already asleep. She lay in bed feeling sorry for herself. My friends like my family better than they like me, thought Francie. And my family feels the same way about them. Francie decided to run away first thing in the morning.

* * *

But the smell of pancakes woke Francie on Saturday morning. Francie thought she might as well run away after breakfast. She put on her fuzzy robe and went downstairs.

Jo Jo was in the kitchen, singing a song to Ernestina. Tobias and Mathias waved their arms and legs at Francie.

"Hello, sleepyhead," said Mom. She gave Francie a stack of pancakes.

Francie was eating the last one when Dad came into the kitchen. "Got a surprise for you, Pumpkin," Dad said to Francie. He lifted her up in his strong arms.

Francie giggled. "Put me down, Dad," she said.

"Nope," he said. "Close your eyes."

So Francie closed them.

Dad carried her out into the backyard. Then he lifted her up onto his shoulders. "Now open them," he said. So Francie did.

She saw a wooden ladder going up into the old pear tree. At the top of the ladder was a little house. "It's the crate the freezer came in," said Dad. "I made it into a tree house just for you."

So that was why Dad had been so busy!

Francie scrambled out of his arms. She climbed up the wooden ladder. She crawled through the door of the tree house.

Dolores was inside. "See the curtains and cushions?" she said. "I made them for you!"

So that was why Dolores had been sewing all the time! Was it a miracle? The tree house was perfect! And it was all hers!

Dolores showed Francie a rope hanging outside the door. "You can swing on this," she said. "And you can slide down. It was Ambrose's idea."

Just then, Ambrose himself ran out into the yard. He was holding a shoe box.

"I found them!" he yelled. "I finally found Romeo and Juliet. Come and see!"

Francie grabbed the rope and slid down to the ground. There in the shoe box were the hamsters. They were cuddled together with their new young family.

"Six new babies!" said Dad. "Aren't they lucky to have such a nice, big family?"

Francie reached up and hugged Dad hard. "*Really* lucky," she said. Her face was shining. "Just like me."